THE AMAZING NINJA BROTHERS

Entering the Deep Unknown

*Celebrating Minds
That Work Differently*

Robert Martin

ROBERT MARTIN
Illustrations by JANE ARCHER

ENTERING THE DEEP UKNOWN
by Robert Martin

While the story, cast of characters, and places are
fiction, the characterization of Attention Deficit
Hyperactivity Disorder is not.

Published by

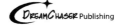

DreamChaser Publishing LLC
RobertMartinAuthor.com

The Amazing Ninja Brothers series is a
registered trademark of DreamChaser Publishing LLC

Cover and Interior Illustration and Design by Jane Archer
Book layout: Nick Zelinger, NZ Graphics

ISBN: 978-0-9908317-6-1 (hardcover)
ISBN: 978-0-9908317-7-8 (softcover)
ISBN: 978-0-9908317-8-5 (eBook)

LCCN: 2018911674

Children's, Attention Deficit Hyperactivity Disorder,
Super Hero, Compassion and Understanding

Printed in the United States of America

First Edition

To all the amazing kids
whose minds work
differently.
~ RRM

Chapter 1

Aiden smothered his laughter as his best friend Tommy tried to balance his pencil on his nose. Aiden glanced toward their teacher, who was busy writing on the board. A couple of kids were starting to giggle.

"Pssst ! Tommy!" Aiden whispered from behind his workbook. "You'd better stop it, or Ms. Strong's going to be annoyed with

you again." Aiden was concerned that his friend sometimes blurted out random things in class. Sometimes he tapped out beats on his desk at inappropriate moments. Tommy could be very funny, but he could also go too far and get into trouble.

Tommy's chair creaked and rocked as his body wiggled back and forth and side to side to keep his balance. "I've almost got it," he yelled.

"Tommy, cut it *out*," said Amanda, from her desk directly behind his. Tommy was losing control, his arms waving recklessly. Other kids started to stare and whisper.

Oh man... thought Aiden.

But it was too late. Tommy lost his balance, and he, his books, and his chair all fell with a thump and a clatter.

"Tommy!" Ms. Strong said firmly, just as the school bell rang. All the kids rose, laughing, talking, and pointing at Tommy.

"Phew. Saved by the bell," said Aiden, bending to help Tommy pick up his things.

"You're always distracting everyone, Tommy," Amanda whined as she squeezed past them. "You're so annoying."

"Yeah," agreed Lincoln, who sat across from Tommy. "It's *really* annoying, dude."

Other kids gave Tommy funny looks as they passed him.

"Ignore them," said Aiden.

But Tommy was off in his own world. "Darn. I almost had it, too." He tapped his pencil on his nose. "I just need a little more practice."

Aiden shook his head. Tommy didn't seem to understand that he had done something wrong. Aiden was silent as they walked through the noisy hallway. Tommy was now babbling on and on about getting a new video game.

They stopped by the school gate.

"When I get it, you have to come over!" Then Tommy finally noticed the look on Aiden's face. "Oh brother, what did I do *now*?" he asked as he stamped his foot and folded his arms across his chest.

"Bud," said Aiden, "you have to stop disrupting the class." He sighed. "I mean, c'mon… Do you *like* it when Ms. Strong gets upset with you?"

Tommy shook his head. "Don't you think I want to sit still like everyone else?"

Aiden shrugged. It sure didn't seem like Tommy wanted to sit still.

"I just can't," said Tommy. "I get so bored when we have to repeat stuff we've already learned. That's when my mind wanders in search of something more interesting or exciting to do. Then I get all antsy."

"Maybe if you just stop fooling around, you'll be able to pay more attention," said Aiden.

Tommy scowled. "Whatever, dude." He frowned and tugged his backpack back onto his shoulder. "Loser," he said under his breath as he stomped away toward his bus.

Aiden winced. "Hey, maybe we can hang out tomorrow after school?" he called.

But Tommy didn't even turn around.

Chapter 2

On the school bus home, Aiden slumped against the window, staring out at nothing. Tommy had been his best friend since kindergarten. They had never had fights, just fun. But Tommy's behavior in class was getting on everyone's nerves.

Aiden felt a tap on his shoulder. "Hey, what's the matter?" asked his younger brother Jacob from the seat behind.

Aiden told Jacob what had happened. "I just don't get why Tommy does that stuff. I get bored in class sometimes, too, but I control myself, you know? It's really not that hard." He sighed heavily. "But now he's mad at me. I was only trying to help him."

Soon, the bus pulled up outside their grandfather's house, where Aiden and Jacob waited until their parents got home from work. They loved that their grandfather's house was right across the street from their own. Their grandfather, Papa, was funny and almost always said yes when they asked for something.

Jacob raced off the bus and into the house knowing that Papa's freshly-baked cookies would be waiting. Aiden moped in a few minutes later and joined Jacob and their grandfather at the kitchen table. Jacob chattered about his day, only stopping to take bites of cookie, but Aiden stayed quiet.

Papa offered Aiden the plate of cookies, saying, "You seem a little sad, Slugger," which was Papa's nickname for Aiden. Papa had a nickname for each of his grandchildren. Jacob's was Scooter.

Aiden sighed. "It's nothing." He took a cookie, but didn't feel like eating it.

"He's just upset about Tommy," Jacob piped up.

"Papa," said Aiden, "Tommy never pays attention. He'll be listening one minute then off juggling erasers or bursting out rapping the next. He gets in trouble with Ms. Strong more and more often. And even when he does pay attention, he fidgets. The other kids think he's weird. It's bugging everybody."

"Even you?" asked Papa.
Aiden shrugged. If he was honest with himself, it was annoying when Tommy messed around as everyone tried to work.

"I guess," he said finally. "It's hard to concentrate when Tommy's goofing off. And even when he isn't goofing off, he still isn't always paying attention. Just yesterday, Ms. Strong had to say his name three times before Tommy stopped daydreaming

She was like, 'Tommy? TOM-mee? TOMMY!"

"Ah," said Papa, nodding slowly. "That *is* a tough one."

"I want to help him," said Aiden. He picked a raisin out of his cookie and squished it on the plate with his thumb. "But I tried, and now he hates me."

"He doesn't hate you," said Papa, touching Aiden softly on the back hoping to comfort him.

Why don't you just ask him to stop?" Jacob wiped the crumbs off his mouth. "That's what Mrs. Perry says we should do when someone's bugging us."

"I tried to do that, but I guess I didn't do it right." Aiden's entire body cringed at the thought of seeing Tommy the next day. Would his best buddy still be angry with him? "I feel like there's nothing I can do to help him. He just doesn't get it." Aiden felt his frustration growing again. Why couldn't Tommy just decide to sit still and pay attention?

Papa sat stroking his chin. After a long moment, he stood. "Boys…" he said slowly, "I think I can help."

"How?" Aiden's heart pounded. Papa looked so serious.

"It's a secret that has been in our family for a very long time," said Papa. "But…"

"What, Papa?" interrupted Jacob.

"But… you **must** promise to keep it secret," said Papa. "You mustn't even tell your best friends, nor your parents - *no* one."

Jacob's eyes opened wide.

Aiden's heart beat faster. "We promise," he said.

"Double triple promise!" said Jacob.

When Papa peered through the front window, Aiden guessed he was making sure Mom wasn't home yet.

"Okay boys, follow me, Papa said quietly.

Chapter 3

In his study, Papa slid an old encyclopedia halfway out of the bookshelf. He reached behind it. When he pulled his hand out, he held a small, carved, red, wooden box. He motioned for the boys to come closer, so he could huddle with them in secrecy.

Papa lowered his head and placed his index finger on his lips. "Shhh, we need to whisper."

Aiden felt like he was going to burst, and Jacob looked like he felt the same. Aiden wished Papa would hurry up.

"Your great-great-grandfather was an explorer," Papa said, keeping his voice low. "One day, while in the Far East, he discovered two special rings." The lid clicked as Papa carefully opened the box. The boys looked around as if expecting someone might hear it. Inside the box were two dull metal rings.

"Now, be careful," said Papa, gently handing one to each of them. "Each comes with its own superpower."

Aiden almost laughed. Superpowers? Papa had to be joking, right? Old and tarnished, with a dull stone set in each, the rings sure didn't look very special.

"What kind of power? Can they make you fly?" asked Jacob, staring wide-eyed at the ring in his palm.

"No," Papa chuckled and placed his wrinkly hand over Jacob's. "I'll tell you about their powers, but before I do, you must both promise to use them only when you *truly* need to."

Papa looked so serious, Aiden was starting to believe these rings must totally be special. "I promise," he said.

"I triple quadruple promise," said Jacob.

"Well" … Papa lowered his voice to a whisper. "It's believed that, long ago, the rings belonged to two ninja brothers—"

"Like real, actual ninjas?" interrupted Jacob, his whisper loud with surprise.

"Shhh," Aiden warned.

"That's right," said Papa. "And they had special powers."

"For fighting?" asked Aiden. He wondered how that could help Tommy.

Papa grinned. "That's what makes these rings so amazing. While ninjas were always known for fighting, these ninja brothers were famous for preventing fights."

"How did they do that?" asked Aiden.

"Back then, feuds were mostly because of misunderstandings. Most often, it was because someone or some group could not understand the actions of another."

"Just like Amanda and others in class don't always understand the things Tommy does," said Aiden.

"Brilliant!" said Papa.

Jacob's eyes went blank. "I don't get it."

"What made the ninja brothers so special," said Papa, "was their ability to find out why a person acted in an unexpected way, one that wasn't appreciated or understood by others. Once they figured out the reason, they could help others understand and find ways to be supportive."

"All because of these junky old rings?" asked Jacob.

Aiden stared at the dull, dark metal and the dingy orange stone. It did look like a piece of junk. Could it really help him help Tommy?

"Yes, because of those rings," Papa said gently. "They might look like junk to you, but just wait. Because of the powers of these rings, the ninja brothers became known for creating understanding and support for those who needed it."

"Just like Tommy," said Aiden.

"Yes," said Papa. "Just like Tommy. Let me explain how it works. I'll start with Jacob, as what his ring does has to happen first. Jacob's job will be to determine what the problem is. Jacob, put your ring on. It will give you the Power of Understanding."

Looking doubtful, Jacob slipped the ring onto his index finger. "What am I supposed to understand, Papa?" he asked.

"In Tommy's case, it is understanding what's causing him to be disruptive in class," said Papa. "It will help you work out why Tommy acts the way he does, Jacob."

Jacob tapped on the dull green stone and frowned as nothing happened. "I think mine's broken."

"Slow down, Scooter," said Papa. "I haven't told you how to use it yet, plus you have to be near Tommy for it to work."

"Oh," Jacob said. His lower lip turned down in disappointment. "So, how does it work, Papa?"

Papa tenderly pulled Jacob closer to him, emphasizing the importance of secrecy. "Turn the stone toward your palm. Make a fist and take three long, slow, deep breaths. Good job, Scooter. Now do that the next time you see Tommy, but don't let him see the ring. It's important that you remember that. Got it?

"I've got it, Papa, and I'm ready to rock

and roll," said Jacob, his infectious enthusiasm back in force. "Your turn, Aiden."

Aiden slipped the ring onto his pointer finger. It felt strangely warm against his skin. "What does mine do, Papa?"

"Your ring will give you the Power of Empathy," said Papa.

"What's empathy, and how will that help Tommy?" asked Aiden.

"It means you feel the same emotion that Tommy feels inside, plus, because of the ring's power, you'll be able help others know how special Tommy really is and help them want to be reassuring and encouraging."

"Amazing!" said Aiden. "Jacob, you can figure out what makes Tommy act the way he does in class, and I'll figure out how to help. Great combination!"

"We're ninjas. Hooray!" said Jacob. "Amazing!" said Aiden.

Papa laughed. "I think that, from now on, I'll call you the Amazing Ninja Brothers."

Now Aiden couldn't wait to see Tommy tomorrow.

Chapter 4

The next morning, Aiden and Jacob waited for Tommy in front of the school as usual. Aiden paced back and forth. His eyes searched everywhere for a sign of Tommy. "What if Tommy doesn't want to be my friend anymore? He was so mad at me yesterday."

"He probably forgot again," said Jacob.

"No, I didn't!" Tommy yelled as he leapt from behind a tree and knocked into them. Aiden landed on the ground with a thud. Tommy's backpack flew across the sidewalk and spilled out its contents.

As he got up and brushed himself off, Aiden saw papers blowing away from the backpack. Tommy lay on the ground laughing hysterically.

"Dude, your homework's getting away," said Aiden.

"What did he do that for?" growled Jacob, as Tommy ran after his homework.

"See what I mean?" said Aiden. "He sometimes doesn't think before he acts."

At least Tommy was no longer mad at him. He seemed to be in good spirits. Tommy was cool like that. Even when he lost his temper, it didn't take long before he was all smiles again.

While Tommy was distracted, Aiden blinked hard twice at Jacob, a ninja signal they had worked out between them.

Jacob gave a little nod and spun his ring around, so the dull stone was in his palm. Looking anxious, he stared at Tommy, made a fist, then squeezed his eyes shut. He started to breathe deeply.

Tommy came back, shaking his homework papers. They were covered in thick, dripping mud.

"Uh-oh. What are you going to tell Ms. Strong?" asked Aiden.

"She's gonna be mad, huh?" Tommy said, using the bottom of his shirt to wipe mud off his homework.

While Tommy was busy, Aiden glanced at Jacob. His brother's eyes were open wide. A vivid green glow radiated between his fingers. Jacob stared at Aiden, a look of shock on his face. Then as the glow faded, he nodded and smiled.

"Um, Tommy?" said Aiden. "I have to take Jacob to… uh… to see the nurse. So, I'll see you in class, okay?"

Tommy stood up. "Okay. Hope you feel better, Jacob."

As he and Jacob walked away, Aiden glanced back. Tommy was still busy picking up his things. Tommy only looked up when Amanda and other kids from the class passed him. It was obvious Tommy could hear them laughing and whispering about him.

Tommy didn't show that his feelings were hurt, but Aiden knew they had to be. Tommy waited a few seconds then trudged into school, following a few steps behind the other kids.

Aiden sighed and then turned to his brother.

Jacob looked worried. "The nurse? Did the ring do something bad to me?"

"No, not at all. It's the first thing I could think of to get us alone fast," said Aiden. He pulled Jacob into the boys' restroom and checked to be sure no one was around. "So… did it hurt? And did it work?"

"Aiden!" said Jacob, his eyes growing wide with wonder. "These ninja rings are magic! First, I got this warm feeling, like heat was flowing straight from my ring, up my arm, and into right here." He poked the middle of his forehead. "Then bam, I could see into Tommy's mind!"

"Whoa!" said Aiden. "What was that like?"

"I don't know how to describe it," said Jacob, shaking his head. "It was wild! Anyway, Tommy is super smart, and his brain is like a racecar; it thrives on speed, needs excitement and can change lanes -

or in his case whatever he is doing - in a split second."

"Makes sense," said Aiden. "That explains why he gets distracted. Except when he's doing something he really likes. He can shoot baskets for *hours*."

"That's because his mind can also be just the opposite, like…" Jacob paused to think. "…like a laser beam. If he likes something, his mind can really focus on it for a long time. Other times, his mind is like an explorer always looking for something more interesting and exciting. When it can't find something, that's when he can't sit still or says something he shouldn't."

"That explains his fidgeting and blurting things out in class." Just then, the school bell rang.

Aiden pushed open the restroom door. "All of this explains why he sometimes doesn't pay attention or follow directions.

And it explains why he does things without thinking them through first."

"Like jumping on us and knocking us over," said Jacob.

"And I'll have the bruises to prove it," said Aiden.

"Your teacher's gonna be so mad about his homework…"

"You bet," said Aiden. "We have to help Tommy—and fast. Let's come up with a plan after school."

Chapter 5

Papa was waiting when the boys burst through the door of his house. "It's the Amazing Ninja Brothers!" he cheered as they raced into the kitchen.

Jacob slid to a stop at the kitchen table. "Papa!" he shouted. "It worked! I can't believe it. The ninja ring really worked! I figured it out! I saw inside Tommy's mind, and it was racing and—"

"Whoa, talk about racing! Slow down there, Scooter," said Papa with a grin. "Now, sit yourself down, catch your breath, and tell me what you now understand about Tommy's actions in class."

Jacob paused and took a giant gulp of the milk Papa had poured for them. "Okay," he said, flopping into a chair. "I found out that Tommy's brain is really super cool and exceptional. It goes at a speed that's faster than a rocket ship. That's why he is so amazing at certain things. But sometimes his speedy brain gets him in trouble. If his brain isn't doing something exciting or interesting, he becomes bored. However, when he does something that gets his brain going, watch out! He'll go after it, leaving whatever it was he was doing."

"And without always considering the consequences," added Aiden.

"Ah, I see," said Papa, nodding. "And how does that make you feel, Slugger?"

"I feel better now that we that know that Tommy can't help it," said Aiden. "Before, I thought he was just being a brat or goofing off to get attention."

"Boys, what Jacob has described sounds like Attention Deficit Hyperactivity Disorder or ADHD. Some of our greatest leaders, scientists, artists, athletes, and other extraordinary people have had ADHD. And I wouldn't be surprised if Tommy becomes extraordinary himself."

"Papa! Papa! Papa!" Jacob said, unable to contain himself. "There is something else I understand about Tommy and why he'll definitely be one of those extraordinary people, too. When he sets a goal, he'll work hard and invent new ways to achieve it. When he's on a team he expects only the best from his teammates. Fairness is really important. When he's not treated fairly, watch out."

"That's my buddy, Tommy," Aiden said. Aiden brushed a tear off his face, hoping the others didn't notice. It was weird that being proud of Tommy made him want to cry, but it did.

Papa smiled. "And what about you, Slugger, did you discover how to help Tommy?"

"Not yet," said Aiden. "But I'll try right now."

"I'm afraid Tommy is just too far away for it to work," said Papa.

"I should have done it at school," said Aiden, frustrated. "I just never got the chance. I never had a time when Tommy and I were on our own. We were so lucky no one saw the glow when Jacob used his ring. It's bright!"

"Yeah," said Jacob. "That would have been tough to explain."

"I'll have to find a time when I'm right up next to Tommy," said Aiden, "but I have to use my ring where no one will see…" He thought for a moment. "I know! Tommy is getting a new video game tomorrow, and he wants me to go play it with him. Maybe we can go to his house after school. Tommy will be distracted by the game. It should be easy to use my ring without anyone noticing."

"I agree," said Jacob. "After all, we are the Amazing Ninja Brothers."

Chapter 6

The plan was all set. The next day, Aiden and Jacob went home with Tommy.

But when Tommy finally revealed which game he'd received and started to load it up, Aiden looked at Jacob, wide-eyed. It was called Ninja Friend Protector. Was it a coincidence? Or did Tommy know something about their powers?

Jacob looked back at Aiden and mouthed the words, "No way could he know."

Aiden relaxed. He knew one of Tommy's other qualities was that he considered it his responsibility to protect his family and friends. His dedication and loyalty to the people he cared about was off the charts.

Perhaps Tommy is the real Ninja Friend Protector, he thought with a smile.

The screen flashed as Tommy chose an avatar and equipped it with armor and weapons. He was totally absorbed. It was time.

Aiden sprang into action. He spun the ring's stone into his palm, then piled cushions over his hand. Heart thumping, he concentrated on Tommy.

With his first deep breath, the river of warmth ran up his arm. Within seconds, it traveled up his neck. With his third breath, it reached the center of his forehead and sizzled with a pleasant buzzing sensation. Aiden smothered a gasp. Bright orange sparkles glowed between his fingers.

There was a bright flash across Aiden's brain and suddenly he could see Tommy's thoughts! Not only that, he could feel Tommy's feelings. Tommy's excitement about his new game burst inside Aiden like fireworks. Tommy's pride at showing his best friends his new game was like a warm buzz inside Aiden. But there was something else, too.

Aiden saw that Tommy was sometimes troubled by worry, sadness, and frustration. They were like schoolyard bullies in his brain. As Aiden traveled through Tommy's brain, he saw some of what troubled his best friend: Ms. Strong becoming annoyed; Amanda hissing, "Be quiet, Tommy;" and the other kids giving Tommy disapproving looks.

Aiden continued his journey in Tommy's brain, feeling what Tommy felt as he traveled. He felt Tommy's anxiety about knowing his brain worked differently to most people's brains. He felt his compassion, his strong sense of fairness, his hurt feelings when kids laughed or talked about him behind his back, and his deep sadness when he disappointed his family and friends.

Aiden also saw Tommy's frustration with homework. Tommy really wanted to complete his homework, but when something more exciting slipped into his mind, it pushed any thought of homework aside.

"Hey, are you guys hungry?" said Tommy suddenly.

Aiden stifled an enormous gulp as the connection to his friend's mind was severed. "Starving!" he managed to say.

"I'll ask Mom for some snacks." Tommy got up and went into the kitchen.

Jacob looked knowingly at Aiden. "Pretty cool, huh?" he said.

Aiden slowly blinked and nodded as his mind cleared. "Yes, and no," he whispered thoughtfully. Aiden was happy that he now could help his friend, but wished he had done so sooner.

"Did you figure out how we can help?" asked Jacob.

"Yes, but you'll be surprised how," said Aiden.

Chapter 7

O n Monday morning, when they arrived at school, the Amazing Ninja Brothers felt hopeful. Aiden had explained to Jacob how bad Tommy often felt. Now they had a double mission: to help other kids see Tommy's great qualities, and to help Tommy feel better about himself.

But even before the bell rang, they could see it wasn't going to be easy. They were in Aiden's classroom, considering their plan, when Tommy slid into the room on his stomach. Then he gave a monstrous roar.

"What's up, guys?" he said, rolling onto his back and laughing.

Aiden and Jacob looked at each other and then at Ms. Strong.

Oh brother, thought Aiden. The school day hadn't even started yet. Was Tommy in trouble already?

"Hi, Tommy," Ms. Strong said with a warm smile. "I love your energy and imagination this morning. Are you a worm or a caterpillar?"

Tommy beamed as he got up. "I'm a Bloob. It's a creature in *Ninja Friend Protector."*

"That sounds like a lot of fun," said Ms. Strong.

"It is! Right, guys?"

Aiden and Jacob nodded enthusiastically, and Jacob looked as relieved as Aiden felt.

Tommy went toward his desk, but as he passed their teacher, he stopped. "Ms. Strong," he said softly, "I promise I'll be super-quiet and good today."

"I know you'll try your best, Tommy," said Ms. Strong in a tone that conveyed warmth and understanding.

Tommy smiled back.

Jacob fist-bumped Aiden and left for his own classroom. Knowing Tommy was going to try to be quiet and focused was comforting. And Ms. Strong was kind and understanding. Things were looking up already.

But as class began, it wasn't too long before Tommy was fidgeting and tapping on his desk with his pencil.

From the desk behind Tommy's, Amanda slammed her hand on her desk. "Shhhh!" she whispered loudly. "You're so weird," she said under her breath.

Aiden knew that if he had heard it, Tommy had, too. He rolled his eyes at his best friend. "Once a pest, always a pest," he whispered.

But Tommy looked upset. "Geez," he grumbled.

Amanda hissed, "I said SHHHHHHH!"

Later, during English Language Arts, when everyone was silently writing, Tommy stared out the window. "What kind of dog is that?" he blurted out. "And why do dogs dig holes anyway? For pooping in?"

Everyone laughed—even Amanda. Ms. Strong shook her head. Aiden shuffled uneasily in his seat, afraid to look at Tommy and see his embarrassment. He didn't need to use his ninja ring to know how his best friend felt.

On the playground at recess, Aiden and Jacob agreed to try and cheer Tommy up.

"What's up, dude?" said Aiden. "Are you okay?"

"Nope," said Tommy. "Everyone thinks I'm annoying and weird. Even you."

"Dude, no way," said Aiden. "Both Jacob and I know you're really smart."

"Sure," said Jacob. "And we understand that your brain works differently."

Tommy looked shocked.

"B-b-but in lots of ways," continued Aiden anxiously, before Tommy could respond. "You're even smarter than the other kids. You're excellent at math. You tell really cool stories. In sports, everyone wants you to be the captain."

"You dance great!" added Jacob.

"Yeah, and you write cool raps!" said Aiden.

At that, Tommy glanced up shyly.

But his expression turned stormy again. "Anyway, how do you know about my brain?" he said.

"I figured it out!" said Jacob, receiving a nudge from Aiden. "I mean, we did. I mean, the Amazing—"

Aiden shot his brother a warning glance, and Jacob fell silent. "We learned something about ADHD from our papa, and we… ummm …. put two and two together," Aiden said.

"There's nothing wrong with me, you know," said Tommy, scowling.

"We know!" said Aiden quickly. Jacob nodded vigorously. "But we just noticed you've been feeling down—"

Just then, he saw Amanda flouncing across the schoolyard toward them, followed by a trickle of other kids. She stopped right in front of Tommy and took a deep breath. "Tommy," she said. "You have to stop."

"What?" said Tommy. "Geez, what did I do now?"

"You purposely annoy me in class."

"I do not," said Tommy. His face was red.

"Hey guys, cool it," said Aiden. "Amanda, he doesn't do it to upset you, I promise."

"I swear," said Tommy.

"How am I supposed to believe you? You do it every single day. You know how it makes me feel!" Amanda's chin trembled, and she looked like she might cry. "I can't concentrate with so much noise and fidgeting."

"I don't mean to!" Tommy's voice was rising now, and more kids were pausing to watch and whisper.

"Well—" Amanda paused and gave a great sniff. "That's all I wanted to say." And with that, she turned on her heel and stomped off, followed by wide-eyed, whispering kids.

Tommy looked at Aiden. "See? You'd be feeling down, too, if everyone thought you were weird!" he yelled at Aiden. And with that, he stormed away, too.

Oh brother, thought Aiden.

"Well, Amazing Ninja Brother," said Jacob, "I think things just took a turn for the worse."

Chapter 8

When Aiden and Jacob got to Papa's that afternoon, he greeted them with freshly-whizzed smoothies and asked, "How are the Amazing Ninja Brothers today?"

"So-so," said Aiden. Together, he and Jacob explained what had happened at school.

"Tommy apologized for yelling at me right afterward," said Aiden. "But I hate seeing him so sad and frustrated. And Amanda seemed really upset, too. I actually felt kinda sorry for her."

"Me too," said Jacob. "But guess what?" Jacob's eyes were bright. "I found out some more stuff about Tommy's ADHD today. I used the ring right outside your classroom this morning," he told a surprised Aiden.

"Are you crazy?" said Aiden. "You could have been seen!"

"Don't worry." Jacob looked pleased with himself. "No one saw. I put my hand inside my backpack and waited till the coast was clear. Anyway, Tommy's mind is super-creative and curious. The littlest movement can distract him—except when he's really focused on something he likes."

"Ah," said Aiden. "That does explain the digging dog incident…"

Papa chuckled. "What's that?"

Aiden told him about the dog they had seen through the window. "Up until then, Tommy was doing great. Then he disrupted the class again. Ms. Strong looked disappointed, and Tommy looked worried when he realized he was in trouble—*again.* But the worst part is he thinks the other kids don't like him. I'm worried he may be right."

Jacob patted his brother's shoulder. "But," he said matter-of-factly, "we Amazing Ninja Brothers now have a firm mission: help everyone see how great Tommy is—"

"Including Tommy himself," added Aiden.

"I'd expect no less from the Amazing Ninja Brothers," said Papa, smiling.

The next morning when he and Jacob met Tommy outside school, Aiden was feeling more hopeful.

Tommy seemed in good spirits. Aiden grinned to himself, happy that Tommy was all right—he never let anything keep him down for too long.

They were starting a new project that would take the rest of the week. "You're each going to design and paint or draw your perfect pet," said Ms. Strong. "You'll each write a creative essay about why it's the perfect pet for you. At the end of the week, you will share your creations with the class."

This was a fun project, and everyone got to work quickly. Aiden figured his perfect pet was a dog. Dogs were always happy to see you. They were loyal, loved being petted, and never got sick of playing.

Tommy had his head down, working hard on his project, which was no surprise. Tommy loved drawing and creative writing, and he was good at them, too. Aiden now understood why Tommy could be extremely focused when he enjoyed something.

All was going well until Mei Li wailed, "Amanda, how could you do that to my painting?"

"It was an accident," said Amanda.

Aiden and other kids stood up to see what had happened. Thick blue poster paint was splattered all over Mei Li's frog drawing.

"Was not," said Mei-Li. "You did it on purpose! You're getting me back because I had a sleepover with Julia instead of you."

Ms. Strong had come over by now. "Girls, why are you shouting?"

"I didn't, Mei-Li!" said Amanda. "I didn't knock it over on purpose."

"Ms. Strong," said Tommy calmly, "I saw the whole thing when I looked up to see how much time I had left to finish my project." Tommy turned to face Mei-Li. "Mei-Li, Amanda didn't mean to spill paint on your work. She simply reached over to borrow a brush from Lincoln, and her elbow knocked the container. It was an accident, not meanness."

"Thank you for telling us what you witnessed," said Ms. Strong. "Is this true, Amanda?"

"Yes, I promise. I'm sorry, Mei-Li," said Amanda. "Truly."

"But what about my painting?" said Mei Li. "It's ruined. I'll have to start over."

"Your perfect pet is a frog, right?" said Tommy. "I like frogs, too. Maybe it can be a poison dart frog. They live in South America. Some are a beautiful blue, and spotty."

Smiling, Ms. Strong pulled a book about amphibians from the bookshelf and showed it to Mei-Li.

Mei-Li instantly brightened. "Whoa... They're so pretty!" she said.

Aiden watched all this in wonder. Tommy didn't need him and Jacob to fix everything, just to be understanding and supportive.

But no one seemed more surprised than Amanda.

"You stood up for me," she said. "Why did you do that? I thought you hated me."

"Because it was fair," said Tommy. "It was just the right thing to do. You didn't mean to knock that paint over, just like I never mean to annoy you."

Aiden held his breath, waiting to see how Amanda would respond.

"You don't?" she said.

"No way," said Tommy. "And I don't hate you, not one bit."

Amanda blinked. She looked suspicious. "Well," she said finally, "thanks." And she went back to her work.

As she walked by Tommy, Ms. Strong leaned down. "Great job, Tommy," she said.

The only one smiling wider than Tommy was Aiden. If they could start to change Amanda's mind, maybe all the kids could learn to appreciate his best friend's quirks.

Chapter 9

The next day, Aiden and Jacob were feeling great. Tommy was back to being his usual bouncy self.

"How'd you make out with the math homework?" Aiden asked Tommy as they approached their classroom. "I thought it was tricky."

"Oh no... I forgot again," said Tommy as they entered the classroom. Then he grinned and elbowed Aiden. "Just kidding! I remembered it, and I did it all! I like it when Ms. Strong is proud of me."

"Hi, Tommy," came a voice from behind them. It was Amanda. She gave Tommy a shy smile as she passed by.

Tommy smiled. "Hey!" he said.

Jacob nudged Aiden and grinned. Jacob stifled a giggle.

They had fifteen minutes before the bell rang, and Ms. Strong was out of the room. Maybe she had gone to the bathroom or the office. The other kids had already arrived, and there was lots of chatter and laughing as they greeted each other.

"Hey, what's that's smell?" said Amanda suddenly.

Just then, the fire alarm began to scream. Everybody leapt up and looked around in shock.

"Drill?" asked Aiden.

"It's smoke!" gasped Amanda.

"Oh no!" screamed Evan. "What do we do?"

"We've gotta get out!" said Juan.

"But the smoke's in the hallway!" said Mahmoud.

Amanda began to cry.

Oh no, thought Aiden, as his little brother, who was about to leave for his own classroom, grabbed his arm. Jacob looked terrified.

In the middle of the chaos, Tommy jumped onto Ms. Strong's desk. Standing tall, he clapped his hands. "One, two, three. Eyes on ME!"

Even over the wailing fire alarm, everyone heard him. They stopped and paid attention immediately.

"This is NOT a drill," said Tommy. "But we know what to do. Line up at the door. No talking. No running. Stay low and quickly

leave the building. Stay calm. Do it just like we've practiced."

Tommy's words were like magic. Now that someone was in charge, everyone quickly lined up at the door and started to silently file out of the classroom and away from the smoke toward safety. Tommy stood by the school's exit door watching to make sure everyone left the building. They hadn't.

"Amanda!" he shouted as he raced back into the building and into the classroom. He was stunned by her look of fear. She seemed frozen, staring wide-eyed at him, her face white and tear-stained.

"You've got this, Amanda," said Tommy softly.

"I can't!" cried Amanda.

"We'll be brave together. Take my hand."

Amanda gulped back a sob and, shaking, took Tommy's hand.

"Awesome, you're doing great," said Tommy, as he led Amanda into the hallway and toward the exit.

Ms. Strong sped around the corner toward them. "I'm so glad you're all right!" she said. "I was in the bathroom on the far side of the smoke when the alarm went off. I had to go outside and around to get back to you!"

Ms. Strong shepherded them out onto the sports field to line up with all the other classes for roll call. Jacob ran up to Aiden and hugged him hard. Then he hugged Tommy, too.

"Tommy rescued us, Ms. Strong," said Aiden. "He took charge right away. He kept us calm and remembered exactly what to do."

"If it hadn't been for Tommy, I don't know what would have happened," said Amanda. "He saved me. He saved us all!"

"You're a true leader, Tommy," said Ms. Strong with tears in her eyes. "I'm SO very proud of you."

Tommy grinned bashfully. "I just remembered what we learned and did it."

"Three cheers for Tommy," said Aiden. "Hip-hip—"

"Hooray!" chorused the class.

And no one cheered louder than Aiden, Jacob, and Amanda.

Chapter 10

The next day, everything returned to normal. It turned out the fire had been very small. The janitor had put it out with an extinguisher before the fire department even arrived.

Once they had discussed the fire, Ms. Strong said, "I think we all deserve to do something fun for the rest of the day! Let's finish your perfect pet projects and share them." Everyone was happy about that!

My PERFECT
PET by TOMMY

SNUFFLE

Aiden had decided his favorite dog was a boxer. Their aunt had one named Baxter, and he was the sweetest, goofiest dog Aiden had ever met. Tommy hummed happily to himself as he worked on his project. Aiden smiled. He hadn't seen his best friend truly happy for a while.

When it was finally time to share, students took turns to read their page aloud while Ms. Strong held up the picture that the student had drawn. Evan had chosen a cat. Maria picked a hamster. Amanda chose a black velveteen rabbit and talked about how soft and quiet it would be. In fact, everyone wrote about actual animals.

Everyone but Tommy.

Tommy's pet had two heads. It had fluffy wings and a long, fanlike tail. And strangest of all, it was rainbow-colored.

At first, the kids all laughed.

Oh brother, thought Aiden.

But then Tommy started to read. No, he didn't read. He rapped it. Tommy had written a poem!

"My Perfect Pet"
By Tommy

My perfect pet is a snuffle,
for snuffles are super fun.
They're great at shooting baskets
and will play until you're done.

A snuffle is much more helpful
than a pet with just one head.
It helps me with my homework
and reminds me to make my bed.

And if one head is sleeping
and I'm feeling quite ignored,
the other head will be awake,
so I am never bored.

A snuffle will make you laugh
and will take on any dare.
A snuffle is bright and sparkly.
That's why it has rainbow hair.

But Snuffles are inquisitive.
A snuffle's brain is curious.
And since a snuffle has two brains,
its questions can make you furious.

Some snuffles get frustrated, too,
and sometimes they get mad.
But when one throws a tantrum,
know it's not trying to be bad.

A snuffle tries hard to be great.
A snuffle just won't quit.
So, if your snuffle tires you out,
just call out, "Snuffle, SIT!"

A snuffle's caring and giving.
A snuffle is kind and fair.
A snuffle is smart and int'rested
And a snuffle likes to share.

My perfect pet is a snuffle
I'll love him until the end.
He might be kind of goofy,
but he'll always be my friend.

"Wow, so cool!" said Simon.

"Great job, Tommy!" said Ms. Strong. "So creative!"

"Now I want a snuffle, too!" giggled Amanda.

"I think I already have one," said Aiden. "A snuffle sounds an awful lot like Tommy."

"Hey, you're right," said Amanda.

Everyone laughed, especially Tommy.

At recess, Aiden found Jacob and told him all that had happened that morning.

"That's awesome! We did it!" said Jacob, fist-bumping Aiden. "I cannot wait until we tell Papa!"

"I'm afraid there is even more to tell Papa. I think we need to use the rings again."

The Amazing Ninja Brothers Have Another Case:

"Entering Hostile Territory"
Coming Soon!

Letter from Tommy

Dear kids of all ages,

Thank you for reading my story. I'm guessing that you might have a classmate like me, whose mind is wired a little differently than yours. If you do, you probably find him[1] lots of fun, but also annoying at times. I can tell you for sure, he doesn't mean to annoy you, and when he sees that he has, he feels bad about himself. I know. I did.

Thanks to Aiden and Jacob (*The Amazing Ninja Brothers*) that all changed. They helped my classmates understand me and how I was feeling, so much so that I now realize some cool things about myself. When we got to write about our perfect pets, my friends and teacher told me I was off-the-charts creative for inventing the snuffle rap song. Then, when there was a scary fire at school and I helped my classmates, everyone said I was a natural born leader. The Amazing Ninja Brothers made me, and everyone else in my class, realize the importance of celebrating minds that work differently.

Thanks to my classmates and the Ninja Brothers, I now have the self-confidence and drive to chase my dreams. I am lucky. There are millions of other kids like me who are not. They need someone to step forward and become their Ninja Brother or Sister. They need someone just like you. Join the celebration of minds that work differently: become a Ninja Brother. Start today! Your friend needs you – big time.

Thank you.

Tommy

P.S. To learn more about being a Ninja Brother, or Sister visit *www.NinjaBrothers.org.*

[1] I've used the masculine pronoun, but girls can have ADHD, too.

Letter from Amanda

Dear kids of all ages,

Tommy is the most loyal and understanding friend I have ever had. It's important to him that I am safe and happy. Although he has always felt that way, it took Aiden and Jacob (*the Amazing Ninja Brothers*) to make me realize it. The same is true for all of his classmates.

Thanks to Aiden and Jacob, our class learned to appreciate the uniqueness of Tommy's mind, and the powerful sensitivities that influence his emotions. We saw firsthand and benefitted from some of the magnificent qualities of a mind that works differently, as did Tommy himself. Because of our belief in him, he gained the self-confidence and drive he needed to chase his dreams.

The Ninja Brothers unveiling of Tommy's true character and potential was like opening a gift whose outer wrapping did not offer much promise, only to find inside a present that would be treasured and enjoyed for a lifetime.

The happiest day of my life, and perhaps our entire class would say the same, was when the Ninja Brothers opened our eyes to the wonder and magic of our fellow classmate, Tommy. I am pretty sure there is someone whose mind works differently in your class. Join the celebration of minds that work differently, become a Ninja Brother or Sister. Start today! Your friend needs you – big time.

Thank you.

Amanda

P.S. To learn more about being a Ninja Brother or Sister, visit *www.NinjaBrothers.org.*

30 Million Kids Need Your Voice! Join the Crusade to Improve Pediatric Research.

Of the 75 million children in the U.S., 30 million struggle everyday with the challenges of a debilititating chronic disease or disorder. We can do better.

Doing a better job of helping children means changing our approach to pediatric research. Despite many well-funded programs, and top minds at work on the problem, the medical breakthroughs these children are counting on have been disappointing. We believe that we can better serve children by connecting the underutilized resources that are already available today. Here's how:

1. *Align and collaborate across institutions and practitioners*
2. *Develop a robust national database for each pediatric disease and disorder*
3. *Include alternative medicine/treatments*
4. *Capitalize on the proven capability of artificial intelligence*

5. Simplify, sensitize and modernize the clinical trial process

The industry agrees that these steps are instrumental to improving pediatric research.

The Bridge to a Cure Foundation's mission is to do just that, to make dramatically improving the pace and success of pediatric research a national priority.

To learn how you can make a difference to the lives of 30 million children, visit the foundation's website, *wwwBridgetoaCure.org.*

Meet the Dream Chaser

As an author and child advocate, Robert Martin is dedicated to inspiring kids to chase their dreams and helping those who can't. He is the author of several children's books, published by DreamChaser Publishing LLC, including two No. 1 Amazon bestsellers.

Martin's books are composed for those among the Seventy-five million children whose dreams have been disrupted by one of life's socialization issues or have had their dreams shattered by a debilitating chronic disease or disorder.

With these children in mind, Martin crafts fast-paced stories that feature characters with a broad range of pediatric health and socialization challenges, including Attention Deficit Hyperactivity Disorder (ADHD), brain cancer and cultural differences. Martin approaches the difficult issues with a child's feelings in mind, showing a keen understanding and sensitivity to their point of view. For a child with a health challenge, the books offer reassurance and a path to courage. For their friends, Martin's storytelling provides a roadmap to understanding and age-appropriate ways to provide support. A teaching guide is provided on Martin's website for each book.

Learn more about Robert Martin, read his articles, and shop for children's books at *www.RobertMartinAuthor.com*.

Follow Robert Martin on Facebook, Twitter, Google+ and Pinterest.

Net proceeds from all book sales go to the Bridge to a Cure Foundation, a nonprofit organization formed to increase the pace and success of pediatric research (*www.BridgeToACure.org*).